Ladybird Readers

My name is Spot!

Series Editor: Sorrel Pitts
Based on the story by Eric Hill

"Hello! What is your name?"

4

"My name is Tom."

5

"Hello! What is your name?"

"My name is Steve."

"Hello! What is your name?"

"My name
is Helen."

"Hello! What is your name?"

"My name is Spot."

"Hello! What is **your** name?"

13

Your turn!

1   **Talk with a friend.** 🗨

Hello!

Hello!

What is your name?

My name is . . .
What is your name?

My name is . . .

2   Listen and read. Match.

1   My name is Spot.

2   My name is Tom.

3   My name is Steve.

4   My name is Helen.

Beginner

978–0–241–31941–3 ☐

978–0–241–31942–0 ☐

978–0–241–31944–4 ☐

978–0–241–31609–2 ☐